Dick King-Smith

Henry Pond the Poet

illustrated by Russell Ayto

D1146588

Text copyright © Foxbusters Ltd. 1989
Illustrations copyright © Russell Ayto 1996

First published in 1989
by Hodder & Stoughton Children's Books
This edition 1996

10 9 8 7 6 5 4 3

The right of Dick King-Smith to be identified as the author
of this work has been asserted by him in accordance
with the Copyright, Designs and Patents Act 1988.

The characters and situations in this book are entirely
imaginary and bear no relation to any real person
or actual happenings.

This book is sold subject to the condition that it
shall not, by way of trade or otherwise, be lent, re-sold,
hired out or otherwise circulated without the publishers
prior consent in any form of binding or cover other
than that in which it is published and without a similar
condition including this condition being imposed
on the subsequent purchaser.

No part of this publication may be reproduced or
transmitted in any form or by any means, electronic or
mechanical, including photocopying, recording or any
information storage or retrieval system without either the
prior permission in writing from the publisher or a licence,
permitting restricted copying. In the United Kingdom
such licences are issued by the Copyright Licensing Agency,
90 Tottenham Court Road, London W1P 9HE.

ISBN 0 340 65700 6

Printed and bound in Great Britain by
Mackays of Chatham PLC, Chatham, Kent

Hodder Children's Books,
a division of Hodder Headline plc,
338 Euston Road,
London NW1 3BH

—Poetic Toad—

Henry Pond was a poet. All the other toads in the neighbourhood were very proud of this fact. When they spoke of him, they never referred to him as just 'Henry Pond', much less plain 'Henry', but always as 'Henry Pond the Poet'.

Toads take their family names from their places of birth, the waters in which they hatched from spawn to tadpole. 'River' is a common surname, as are 'Lake' and 'Pool' (though a few families affect double-barrelled names such as 'Mill-Pool' or 'Duck-Pond'). 'Pond' is, in fact, probably the commonest of all, but Henry's gift, everyone agreed, was most uncommon.

everyone croaked whenever his name was mentioned, and they never missed an opportunity to mention it, loudly, in front of such lesser creatures as frogs and newts.

Two toads might be sitting side by side,
saying nothing, simply staring vacantly
out of their bulgy golden eyes, when a
frog would chance to hop past.

Immediately they would
start a loud conversation
between themselves.

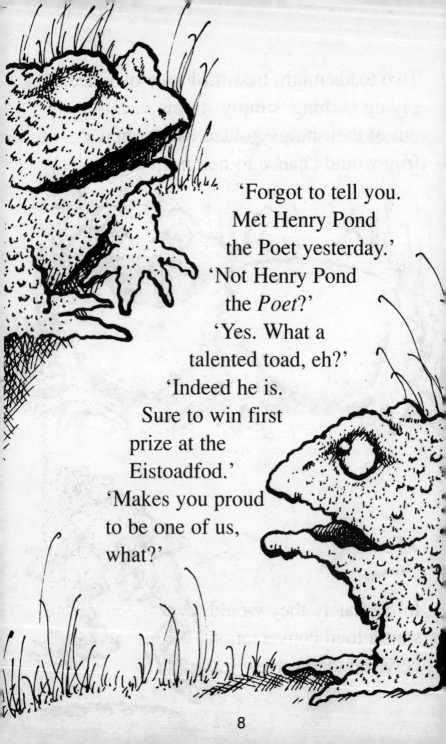

'Forgot to tell you.
Met Henry Pond
the Poet yesterday.'
'Not Henry Pond
the *Poet*?'
'Yes. What a
talented toad, eh?'
'Indeed he is.
Sure to win first
prize at the
Eistoadfod.'
'Makes you proud
to be one of us,
what?'

And then the frog would say
(in a tone of amazement),

A poet?
A toad that
makes up
poems?

And the toads would reply,

Hop it, frog-face.
We weren't croaking to you.

And then they would sit in happy silence
again, waiting for another passer-by and
another chance to sing the praises of
Henry Pond the Poet.

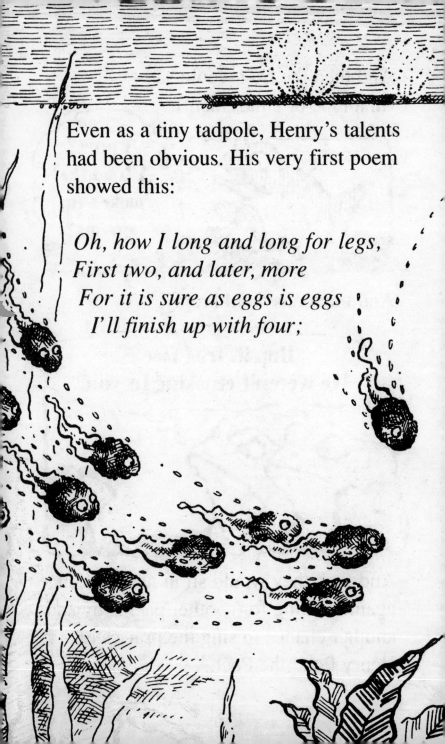

Even as a tiny tadpole, Henry's talents had been obvious. His very first poem showed this:

Oh, how I long and long for legs,
First two, and later, more
For it is sure as eggs is eggs
I'll finish up with four;

And I shall give three rousing
*   cheers*
To see my tail grow shorter,
Till toadally it disappears
And I can leave the water.

Henry would recite this poem to all
his thousands of fellow tadpoles (or
toadpoles, as he called them in his
poetical way) as they swam about the
pond together.

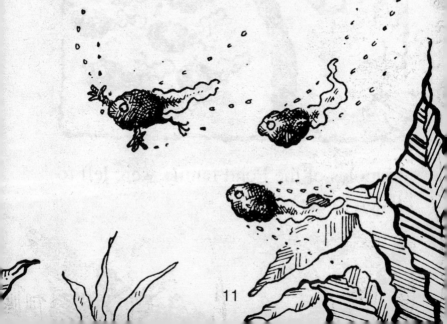

11

But ducks, newts, fish and water-beetles reduced their numbers severely, and day by day fewer . . .

and fewer . . .

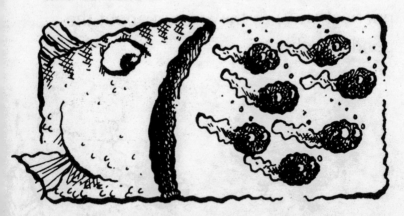

tadpoles of the Pond family were left to listen to the poem.

At the two-legged stage, hundreds heard it, at the four-legged stage, dozens only; and by the time their tails had disappeared and they were ready to emerge from the water as toadlets, only a handful remained to hear the latest work of Henry Pond the Poet.

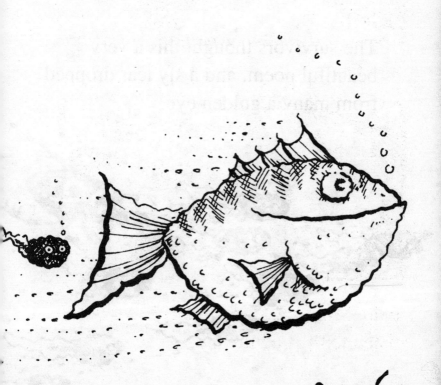

Remember now our friends of yore
That vanished down the fish's maw,
Or in the water-beetle's jaw,
Or duck's webbed paw, or newt's
  sharp claw.
Though they have passed through
  Death's dark door,
They are not lost, but gone before.

The survivors thought this a very
beautiful poem, and a sly tear dropped
from many a golden eye.

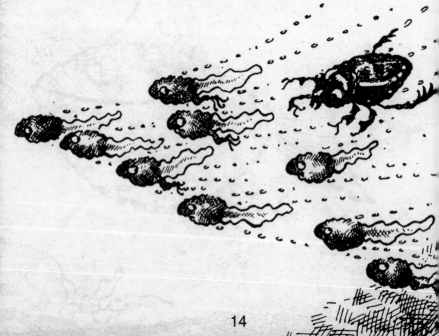

Before long, however, many a golden eye closed, never to reopen, because its owner had not listened carefully enough to the next composition of Henry Pond the Poet:

Now, nevër speak to strangers -
A crow, a snake, a rat -
For life is full of dangers,
And cows will squash you flat;

And flatly you'll be sorry
If you should cross the road:
It doesn't take a lorry
To pulverise a toad.

— Lovelorn Toad —

Not all of Henry's poems were gloomy.
Now, as he grew to toad's estate and
put away tadpolish things, he began to
experience the pleasures of grown-up
life, and a good deal of his poetry was
full of joy.

It was at about this stage that he began
to be spoken of for the first time -
among the Rivers, the Lakes, the Pools
and other toad families - as Henry Pond
the Poet.

By now he was living in an old stone shed, a splendidly dark, damp, snail-filled pad he shared with several other young bachelor toads, and it was here that he began his poetry recitals.

Regularly each month, at the time of the full moon, a large company of local toads would assemble to hear the poet croak his latest piece and to enjoy many of the old favourites.

Poems about food were always popular
(and to appreciate this one, you must
realise that every toad can draw its eyes
down into its head, and thus squash its
prey between the bottom of the eyeballs
and the tongue):

Oh, worms are nice and slugs are
  nice
And the centipedes and the old
  woodlice,
But search as you may o'er hill and
  dale,
There's nothing as nice as a big fat
  snail.

And each verse was followed by a
rousing chorus:

Fee fi fo fung!
Squeeze your eyeballs on your
* tongue!*
Fung fo fi fee!
Squash a slimy snail for tea!

Beetles are nice and bugs are nice
And a litter of wriggling baby mice,
But search as you may o'er dale and
* hill,*
A big fat snail's the nicest still.

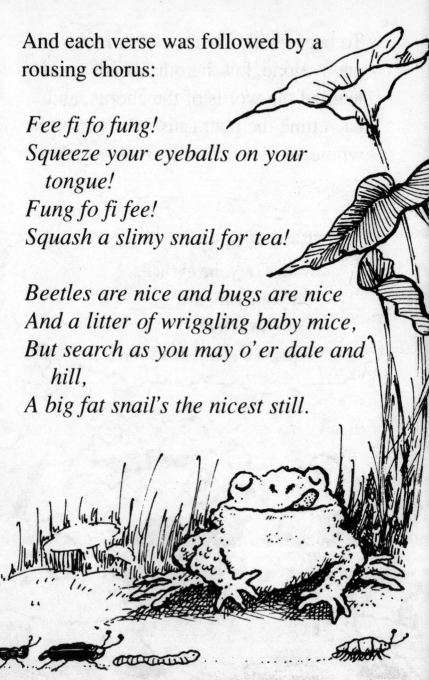

To begin with, Henry would recite this poem alone, but the other toads soon learned the words of the chorus, and each time the poet finished a verse, the whole audience would croak together:

Fee fi fo fung!
Squeeze your eyeballs
on your tongue!
Fung fo fi fee!
Squash a slimy snail for tea!

It was, in fact, at one of these full-moon recitals, just as the sound of that chorus died away, that Henry Pond the Poet fell in love.

She was squatting in the front row, her wide mouth slightly open, her golden eyes fixed upon him; she was hypnotised, it seemed, by his poetry.

Henry delivered himself of a final set of
verses, and then, as the audience began
to crawl away, hastily consulted one of
his friends.

'Who is that amazingly lovely girl
in the front row?'
he whispered.

'Oh, that's Victoria Garden-Pool'
said his friend. 'Tadpole of her year,
she was, and considered to be a great
beauty now that she's come out.'

With fast-beating heart Henry
approached the great beauty. She was
thickly covered, he could see, with the
most delightful warts. Her eyes were
half closed now and her mouth hung
wider still.

Henry, supposing her to be overcome with ecstasy at his recital, was about to speak, when suddenly she yawned, opened her eyes and said, 'Is it finished?'

'Yes,' said Henry. 'Did you enjoy it?'

'Enjoy it?' croaked Victoria Garden-Pool. 'I have seldom spent such a boring evening. Who on earth was that person spouting all that rubbish?'

Henry opened his mouth to say 'Me' and then, realising that she did not recognise him, replied, 'That was Henry Pond the Poet.'

'He seems very fond of the sound of his own voice,' said Victoria Garden-Pool. 'Poets are all the same, I suppose - wet and windy like the weather. Myself, I prefer toads of action,' and she turned her warty back on Henry and waddled out.

'Wait!' called Henry, crawling hastily after her, but when he got outside he could see that there was a toad waiting for Victoria, a burly muscular fellow who looked very much a toad of action. Henry consulted his friend again.

'Who's that?' he said.

'That,' said his friend, 'is Larry Lake.'

'They say that when he was a tadpole, he fought off a minnow.

'And he's been known to eat a full-grown mouse, tail and all.

'He's crawling out with Victoria. I shouldn't tangle with him, if I were you.'

'Oh,' said Henry Pond the Poet.

'Oh dear,' and he watched sadly as the couple disappeared into the night.

Tough Toad

In the weeks that followed, as the moon waned and waxed again, Henry could think of only one thing; would Victoria come to his next poetry reading? It didn't seem likely, but maybe Larry Lake would bring her - if he was fond of poetry, but that didn't seem likely either. Just in case, however, Henry worked hard at composing a new poem. It was a love poem, in which he would pour out his heart as he squatted before her, gazing into her eyes, croaking to her and her alone. He finished it just before the moon was full again:

Come swim with me and be my love -
The fish below, the birds above -
Come swim with me from shore to
    shore
And be my love for evermore!

Come hop with me across the vale,
We'll feast on worm and slug and
    snail!
Come, fairest toad that e'er I saw,
And be my love for evermore!

Come crawl with me along the strand,
Sit by the water, hand in hand,
And dream of joys that lie in store
And be my love for evermore!

But, alas, when his audience gathered
once again to hear the latest works of
Henry Pond the Poet, Victoria Garden-
Pool was not amongst them.

Henry did not feel he
could recite his new
love poem. It was for
her and for her only.
But - in case she did not
come he had prepared
another new poem of
quite a different type.

Since Victoria had
declared her liking for
toads of action, Henry
had been trying hard to
convince himself that
he was one.

He practised blowing
himself up to look
large and terrifying,
and making clumsy
hops at imaginary
enemies.

You may fancy
yourself as a real
he-toad, Larry Lake,
he said to himself,
but Henry Pond is
not just a poet,
you know. He too
is a toad of action!
And his new poem
was designed to tell
this to his listeners:

Who is bold and strong and rough?
Shout it out! You know it!
Who is brave and fierce and tough?

and then (he thought)
they will all say:

Henry Pond
the Poet!

But that evening, once he had seen that Victoria Garden-Pool was not present, and therefore tried out the second of his two new poems, things did not turn out as he had hoped.

Who is bold and strong and rough?
(he said)
Shout it out! You know it!
Who is brave and fierce and tough?

and a voice at the back croaked:

Larry Lake!

'No, no!' said Henry
rather testily. 'You should
have said "Henry Pond the Poet".
"Poet" rhymes with "know it".
"Larry Lake" doesn't rhyme with
anything. Who was the stupid person
who said that?'

At this, there was a disturbance in the audience. A burly muscular toad was bullocking his way through them, shouldering them out of his path until at last he squatted face to face with Henry.

'I was that stupid person,' said Larry Lake.

'Oh,' said Henry Pond the Poet. 'Oh dear.'

'And since you're so rough and tough,' said Larry,

Toads are cold-blooded creatures
anyway, but Henry's blood ran even
colder now. 'What for?' he said.

'That's what I'm going to give you,'
said Larry Lake. 'I'm going to give you
what for. I saw you making eyes at my
lady friend, don't think I didn't. Now
I'm going to give you
a good hiding.'

For a moment the audience was silent,
stunned by this sudden drama in the midst
of a recital.

Then they began to realise that watching
a wrestling match might be a nice change
from listening to poetry, and they started to
move out in a body, carrying Henry and
Larry along with them.

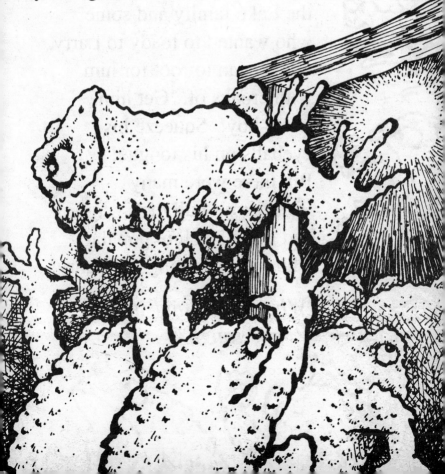

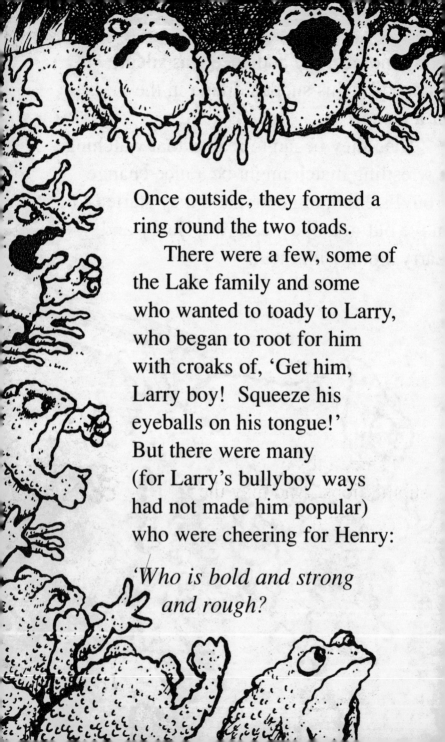

Once outside, they formed a
ring round the two toads.
   There were a few, some of
the Lake family and some
who wanted to toady to Larry,
who began to root for him
with croaks of, 'Get him,
Larry boy! Squeeze his
eyeballs on his tongue!'
But there were many
(for Larry's bullyboy ways
had not made him popular)
who were cheering for Henry:

'Who is bold and strong
*   and rough?*

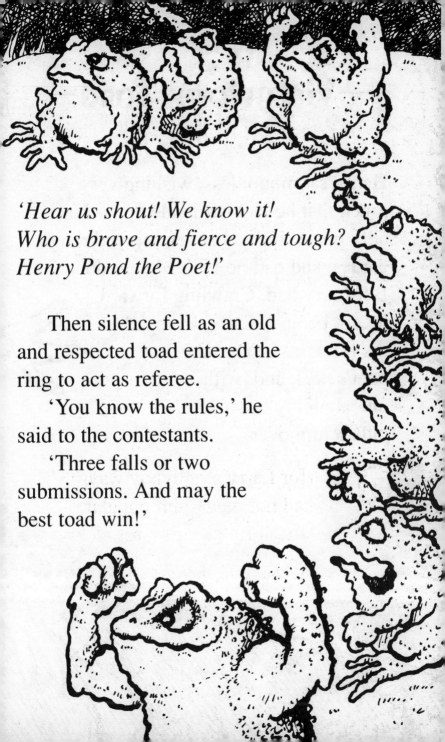

'Hear us shout! We know it!
Who is brave and fierce and tough?
Henry Pond the Poet!'

Then silence fell as an old
and respected toad entered the
ring to act as referee.

'You know the rules,' he
said to the contestants.

'Three falls or two
submissions. And may the
best toad win!'

—Victorious Toad—

Henry sat motionless, wishing very
much that he had not made up such a
silly poem. He had never enjoyed rough
games, and had no idea what to do.
But Larry had. Crawling forward,
he got behind Henry, wrapped
his forearms around the
poet's neck and, with
one almighty heave,
pulled him over
on to his back.

Henry lay kicking
helplessly, while
above the noise
of the crowd,
the referee called,

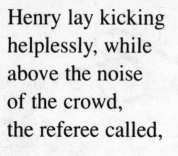

Fall Number One!

Larry Lake sat
waiting for Henry
to right himself.
I wish the Garden-
Pool girl was here,
he thought, to see
me make a mess
of this wimp - and
at that moment he
caught sight of her
crawling up to the
ringside, attracted
by all the noise.

The sound of his beloved's name made Henry turn his head to look at her and, as he did so, Larry Lake took a large hop forward . . .

and butted him under the chin.

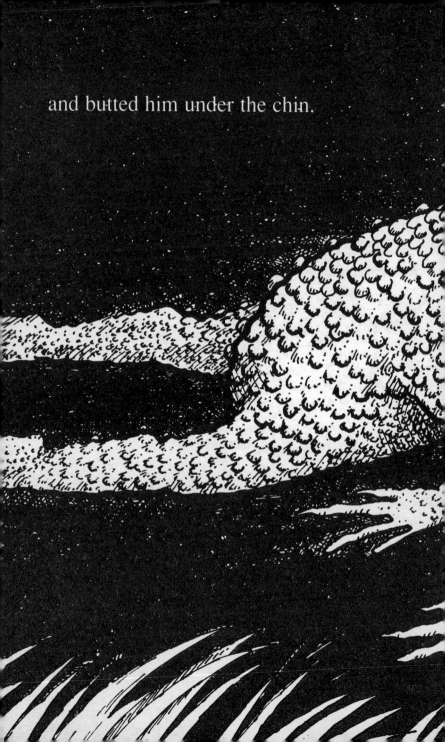

Once again Henry fell
flat on his back.

Fall Number Two!

called the referee.

The Lake supporters were jubilant!
One more fall and the match was
Larry's.

Easy! Easy!

they began to chant,

while Henry's fans were gloomily silent
as their toad struggled to his feet once
more.

They waited for what seemed the certain
end to the fight.

Larry Lake waited, his face split in a sneering grin.

Victoria Garden-Pool waited, her golden eyes fixed upon the toad of action.

she called. She did not spare a glance
for the poet.

Henry waited too, for his head to clear,
and when at last it did, he found, rather
to his surprise, that he was very angry.
Who is brave and fierce and tough? he
asked himself. Why, I am!

And crawling swiftly towards
Larry Lake, he suddenly
shot out his large flat
pink sticky tongue
and hit his opponent
in the eye.

As Larry reeled,
half-blinded,
Henry hit him
in the other one.

Then, nimbly, he grabbed one of Larry's long hind legs and began to bend it the wrong way, harder and harder, until at last the toad of action beat helplessly on the ground with a forepaw in token of defeat.

'Submission Number One!' called the referee.

Henry waited, sportingly, until Larry had cleaned his eyes, but though he was still, his mind was racing.

I mustn't let him close with me, he thought, he's much stronger and heavier. But he's slow. I must keep out of his way, wear him down, tire him out.

And that is exactly what happened. Henry side stepped every leap and lunge that Larry made, ducked under every hop, slipped out from every attempted grasp.

Until at last the big toad sat exhausted, puffing and blowing in the middle of the ring.

Then Henry heard a single voice above the noise of the crowd, a voice that was heavenly music in his ears.

called Victoria Garden-Pool, and at that he leaped upon his enemy's broad back, and got him in a full nelson,

and pressed down with supertoadish
strength until at last, in a strangled
broken croak, Larry Lake cried,

and the referee, hopping forward, raised
high in victory the paw of Henry Pond
the Poet.

Much later that night, Henry and Victoria sat by the water, hand in hand, and the words of the poet floated out over the moonlit ripples:

Come swim with me and be my love -
The fish below, the birds above -
Come swim with me from shore to
    shore
And be my love for evermore!

Come hop with me across the vale,
We'll feast on worm and slug and
    snail!
Come, fairest toad that e'er I saw
And be my love for evermore!

Come crawl with me along the strand,
Sit by the water, hand in hand,
And dream of joys that lie in store,
And be my love for evermore!

'It's funny,' said Victoria. 'When I first heard your poetry, I didn't think much of it. But I do like that one. Am I really the fairest toad you ever saw, Henry?'

'You are,' said Henry.

'In that case,' said Victoria, 'I think I should rather like to be your love for evermore.'

And then she heard the shortest of all Henry's many compositions.

'*Oh, Victoria! I adoria!*' said Henry Pond the Poet.